# Emma's Mystery

Sophia Kazilbash

To order additional copies of this book, contact:
Xlibris
844-714-8691
www.Xlibris.com
Orders@Xlibris.com

ISBN:        Softcover          978-1-6641-6323-2
             EBook              978-1-6641-6322-5

Print information available on the last page

Rev. date: 07/16/2021

I dedicate my book to my grandma Shamshad Rizvi (late) who always been cheering me on and encouraged me in whatever hobbies and businesses I put my hand to. I love you nano.

# Emma's Mystery

# 1
## chapter

Hello, my name is Emma. I'm a police officer. *Ring* . . . I picked up my phone, it was my partner Bob: "Hurry there's been a robbery at the National Bank." I grab my coat and keys hurried out of the house locked the door and got in my car and drove to the crime scene.

When I got there, Chief gave me a badge to enter the scene. When I stepped in, I saw caution tape everywhere, three men being interrogated, all cash registers emptied, and broken handrails for the money vault. It was completely empty, not even one dollar in there. I asked my partner: "How long they were in here," He replied, "About five minutes." Straightaway I knew it was a multi person robbery because it was not possible for one man to do all of that in just five minutes. I also saw a spray paw print. My partner replied, "It is the mark for the Drake brothers." Drake brothers, a group of four brothers who commit crimes together. They make that sign whenever they commit a crime.

I suddenly found an error in my partner's theory. I told him that one of the brothers died in a car crash. My partner said: "He never knew that one of the brothers died." But I told him it was okay that he didn't know. After I left the scene, I gathered all my information and took it to Chief and told him my theory that the Drake brothers robbed the bank. Chief agreed.

That afternoon, I went to get some coffee, and I saw Bob at the back parking lot of the building talking with someone on the phone and screaming at them, but I ignored him and went home. I was relaxing on my couch and remembered the crime scene and how strange Bob was acting. He didn't remember that one Drake brother died. It was on the news on the radio and in the newspaper. Everyone was talking about it at the police station.

Then I realized that Bob started his job one day after Mark, the Drake brother, died. I thought for one second could Bob be the fourth Drake brother Mark, who faked his own death so everyone would think that he was dead. But why would he do that, I thought. Anyway, I didn't trust what I was thinking, so I forgot about my theory. But just to be on the safe side, I should ignore him and shouldn't listen to his advice.

So I got on my computer and typed when Mark Drake died. I got the information; it said that he died on October 7, 2019. Then I signed into police officer records and typed in my password and searched for Bob's records. It said he got hired for the job on October 8, 2019, then I searched if he had any history for jobs. It was blank. Then I checked if he had experience being a police officer. It was blank. I knew it. Bob was the fourth Drake brother, but I wasn't going to Chief or anyone until I was completely sure that I was correct. I need more information and clues, and especially, I should not tell Bob—or should I say, Mark.

Then it hit me. I think I know why Mark faked his death. Because now Mark has a job as a police officer, he could get a lot of information, like go in other people's records, hack into their personal information, and he could go to the crime scene and cover all the clues so it would not point out that it was the Drake brothers. That's why I could find only minor clues.

# 2
## chapter

Meanwhile, back at the parking lot behind the coffee shop, Bob was talking on the phone to the Drake brothers. He was telling them that they needed to step up their game because he thinks his partner Emma was on to them. They thought about another crime. They wanted to break into the jewelry store. He told them they have the rarest diamond of all time and lots of gold, silver, and gemstones. They started to plot how they were going to get in and steal the diamond.

The next day I went to the police station. Suddenly, the chief said on the loudspeaker there's been a robbery at the jewelry store. I rushed into my car and drove to the crime scene. But when I got there, Bob was already there. I was surprised how he got there so fast; he wasn't even at the station today. How did he know there was a robbery here?

Anyway, I went to the scene of the crime. There was caution tape around the stand of the diamond, but there was no diamond because the thieves stole it. The store owner was being questioned. He told me that there were four men wearing black clothes and their faces were covered. "Thank you for your time," I said to the owner. Then I saw a spray paw print. Then it hit me. It was the Drake brothers. Of course, that's why Bob came here so hurriedly. He committed the crime and then came to the crime scene so quickly. I can't believe it. No one noticed that Bob was missing, not even Chief.

A few hours later, I went to the chief and told him about my theory that the Drake brothers did it. The chief agreed. He also saw the spray paw print. I still had one question left: how did Chief never realize that Bob was always at the crime scene before the police but doesn't always come to work? And why doesn't Chief know that he has no history of being a police officer? Why did he hire him?

Sooner or later I knew I had to tell someone about my theory, so I called my sister, Emily. She is also a police officer but in a different police department. I asked her if she could help me with something, but I couldn't tell her on the phone because it was top secret. Emily said that she would be there in one hour.

*Knock, knock!* Someone was at the door, but first I looked out through the peephole. It was Emily. "Hurry, hurry!" I said to her, "Come inside." I took Emily's bag and put it aside. I asked her to follow me. First, I took her to bookshelf. The third row, last book to the right. I pulled it down. I held Emily's hand and off we went, down a five-foot drop, and landed in a ball pit. I told Emily I put it there for safe landing.

I showed her around. There were three computers and paperwork everywhere. Anyway, I told Emily about my theory. The fourth Drake brother is not dead. He is my partner Bob. I showed her all of my evidence, clues, and research. Finally, I convinced Emily the Bob is the fourth Drake brother. She was shocked. She said, "We should go to the chief and tell him." I told her, "Not now because we still need more proof." Emily agreed with me.

# 3
## CHAPTER

The next day Emily stayed at my house and did some research, and I went to the station. Bob was not there. A few seconds later, Chief announced that there has been a robbery at the City Bank. I rushed to the crime scene. Bob was already there. I ignored him. I saw the spray paw print. Then I knew it was the Drake brothers. Then I went to the back of the building to get some fresh air. I saw something behind the garbage can. It was a black mask, black shirt, and black pants. It was the same description the man told me at the jewelry store robbery.

Then it struck me. I knew how Bob got here so early. First, he committed the crime, went to the back of the building, took off the black clothes, and went back in the building to wait for the chief.

I took a zip lock bag and carefully put the mask in there and went back inside and told the chief I had to go to an appointment. He allowed me to go, and I came back to my home and showed the mask to Emily. I wanted to see if my theory was correct, so Emily and I went to the police lab. While Emily was running the DNA check to see if it was Mark's mask, I went to the police station and secretly put a tracking device on

Mark/Bob's coat and quickly went back to my sister. She completed the DNA scan. It was Mark's mask. Then we quickly went back home without informing Chief.

When we reached back home I told Emily that I had put a tracking device on my partner, Bob. I turned on my phone and showed her the red dot. He was headed for the countryside mountain caves.

Then Emily and I got in my car and we followed the red dot to the cave. But when we got there, Bob and the Drake brothers had already left. The tracking device had gone out of range, but we found footprints. They led to the back of the cave, and there was a small box over there. I opened it and there was a hologram that popped up. It was a map of the city and marked places they'd robbed. One mountain not very far from here had a check mark on it. I told Emily that they must have forgotten it when they were leaving cave. Anyway, I took the small device home. Emily did some research on the small device. She found out that they left that device at exactly 4:00 p.m., and we reached there at exactly 4:05 p.m. That's why we missed them. They were in such a hurry, they might have forgotten it. That sounded reasonable.

The next chilly day Emily and I wanted to get a little break from this investigation, so we went skating that day at City Hall Park. We rented some skates and helmets and put them on and started skating for one hour. I thought I saw someone familiar, and it was my partner Bob and the Drake brothers. They were running to their car. One of them had a sack on his back. I told Emily and we quickly skated off the rink and returned the skates. But when we reached the place where the car stood a few minutes ago, it was gone. We missed them again. But they dropped something, looks like it was some kind of diamond crystal. We went home.

Emily and I did some research on the diamond and we found out that it was a piece accidentally chipped off from the diamond. I thought it must have fallen out of the sack the Drake brothers were carrying. The diamonds that were stolen from the jewelry store robbery.

Later that day, the chief called me to the station. He said that a man had spotted four men with the same description the jewelry owner told us. Black masks, black shirts, and black pants. They were headed downtown in a creepy abandoned alley. The chief told me to follow them. Of course, I didn't go alone. I told Emily what Chief said to me. She was interested, so she came with me.

We got in the car and drove very fast since last time we tried to catch the Drake brothers and again we missed them when we got to the location. Chief called me and told me that there has been a robbery at the jewelry store. I was so shocked because he just sent me here. Anyway, I dropped Emily at my house and went to the crime scene. I saw a spray paw print. I was confused because Chief told me someone saw the Drake brothers Downtown and I knew they were here. Anyway, I asked the jewelry store owner if the description of the men was the same. He said, "Yes." I gathered all my clues and informed Chief about my theory about the Drake brothers. Chief said that it was impossible. The Drakes were Downtown, but I said that there was a spray paw print.

"I guess you are right," Emily said to me over the phone. Those four men Downtown could be anyone. It might have been a misunderstanding.

# 4
# chapter

A few days passed and the Drake brothers weren't committing any crimes, so I asked Chief if I could have a week off. Chief allowed me to. When I came home, I told Emily the good news that I got a vacation for one week. Emily had a good idea; she was already on vacation for the week. She said, "Why don't we travel to England?" I agreed to her idea. There are so many sights in England I wanted to see. Like the Birmingham Palace, Madam Tussauds Museum, and the London Eye.

The next day we bought flight tickets to England. That night we packed our suitcases and drove to the airport. When we got to the airport, we waited in line for thirty minutes until we got to the front. They asked for our passports and then asked for our tickets. After we gave them our tickets, we gave them our suitcases, and they loaded them on the plane.

Our tickets showed our flight was at 10 a.m. at Terminal 3. Our flight number was P 24. It was 9.30 a.m. We had still thirty minutes, so we sat on the benches. And when they announced flight number P 24 was now boarding, we got on the plane. The flight attendant looked at our tickets and let us board the flight. Then we found our seats and we were sitting next to each other as our seats numbers were B2 and B3. We sat down.

I noticed that four men with their bags also boarded the plane and they were sitting together. The strange thing Emily and I noticed was that when the air hostess asked them to put their bags in the overhead bins they refused and kept their bags all the time in their laps. Looks like they had strange accents and something was on their faces, but we couldn't figure it out.

It was a six-hour flight. "Here we come," said Emily. Three hours passed and Emily was sleeping. I was watching a movie and in ten minutes was dinner. I woke up Emily and the flight attendant was walking by us and asked me and Emily what we wanted to eat. The air hostess told us about the menu and there were two options: a burger or spaghetti. We chose spaghetti. When we got our food, it tasted horrible, but Emily and I were hungry, so we ate it anyway.

Another strange thing about the four men was that they didn't even use the washroom during the six-hour flight. The pilot announced on the speakers that the plane will be landing in twenty minutes. Emily and I packed our stuff and plane landed. Emily and I got off the plane.

We got our suitcases and called for a cab. We gave the address where we wanted to go to the cab driver. He drove us to the hotel Emily booked for us. When we reached the destination, we paid the driver thirty euros.

The hotel was so big and beautiful from the outside. When we entered, it looked even more beautiful and big. We went to the front desk and asked where our room was. The lady receptionist told us that our room was 2301 and they gave us the keys to the room.

We walked down the hallway and found the elevator. Emily pressed the button for the twenty-third floor. We entered the room. It was a beautiful suite with nice furniture, and it was so big. There was a living room, a kitchen, a bathroom, and two bedrooms. We put our stuff in the bedrooms. We didn't realize that it was 10:00 p.m. It was late and it was really dark outside, so we decided to go to sleep.

# 5
## chapter

The next day, we were awake. It was a bright sunny day. We were hungry but we didn't want to place an order at the restaurant downstairs. I searched for fast food places in the area. There was one nearby and the shop was called Coffee shop. They have breakfast, lunch, and dinner.

We opened the door and there were some benches and a sign that said "Please wait to be seated." So Emily and I had a seat. After a few minutes a waiter came and seated us at booth no. 7 and gave us a menu. I ordered a cheese and egg omelet with avocado toast. Emily ordered a pepper and cheese egg omelet. It took a few minutes to get our breakfast. It was good, really delicious. Emily asked the waiter for some napkins, but it was taking so long. So Emily went to the back.

Next to the kitchen she saw the workers were pulling off their faces but turns out they were taking off their masks. There were four boys—the Drake brothers. The way they were talking, they had the same accent as those four men who were on the plane. But there was one brother missing,

Bob, AKA Mark, who was working at the police station undercover as a police agent.

Emily told me, "Emma, quickly. Hurry, we've got to go. I'll explain everything to you back at the hotel." I didn't know what was going on, so I quickly put some money in the folder and put stuff in my purse, then Emily and I called a taxi.

We quickly arrived at the hotel. We got in our room. Emily quickly closed the door, pulled all the curtains closed to make sure no one was listening, and told me what happed in the restaurant. The Drake brothers are here. Why are they even here? I thought they only committed crimes in Canada. I was thinking if they are in London, then there must be something here that they came for.

Emily searched for anything big going on around here. She found out there was a giant diamond moving from Egypt. The government found the diamond in Egypt when they were doing research inside a pyramid. They were bringing the diamond to the museum on Thursday. "Emily, what day is today?" I asked her. She said, "Today is Tuesday, Emma." "I have an idea. Maybe we should call Chief and he could call the chief of police in London."

So that's what we did. I called Chief and told him what happened in the restaurant today. He said that he would talk to the chief of police in London. He said he would call us back in five minutes. So we waited. In five minutes the chief called me back. He said to me that he spoke to the chief of police in London and they would put more police officers at every exit and beside the diamond. Chief said that there was nothing to worry about. We were going to catch the Drake brothers.

The next day, Emily and I stayed at the hotel in the morning. I turned on the news channel and the breaking news was that the Drake brothers had been spotted in London, but no one knows why there here and what they are doing here. "Emily," I shouted. "Come here, look what's on the news." "What! How did the reporter get the news? How did they find out?" "Maybe Chief told them?" Emily was shocked.

The next day, we wanted to have some fun though we were worried about the Drake brothers' presence in London. Emily and I decided to go to the London Eye, so we went over there. It is a giant Ferris wheel, but first we needed to buy tickets, then we waited in line for twenty minutes before we got on.

When we got to the top, we saw shops, buses, and even Big Ben. After the London Eye we went to Madame Tussauds wax museum. In the museum there were wax figures of famous actors, singers, sports players, presidents, and queen. As we went inside the museum, we saw it was so huge. We saw wax figures of so many famous people and we even got to take pictures with them.

After Madame Tussauds we went to Buckingham Palace and we saw it from outside. There were so many guards around the palace. After we finished seeing Buckingham Palace we went back to the hotel. Emily and I were exhausted from walking so much. We ordered a large cheese pizza. The pizza place's customer service mentioned that to deliver pizza to our door would take ten minutes. After ten minutes, the delivery guy delivered the pizza. After he left, Emily and I ate some pizza. Around twenty minutes later, we both were so full and tired, so we went to bed.

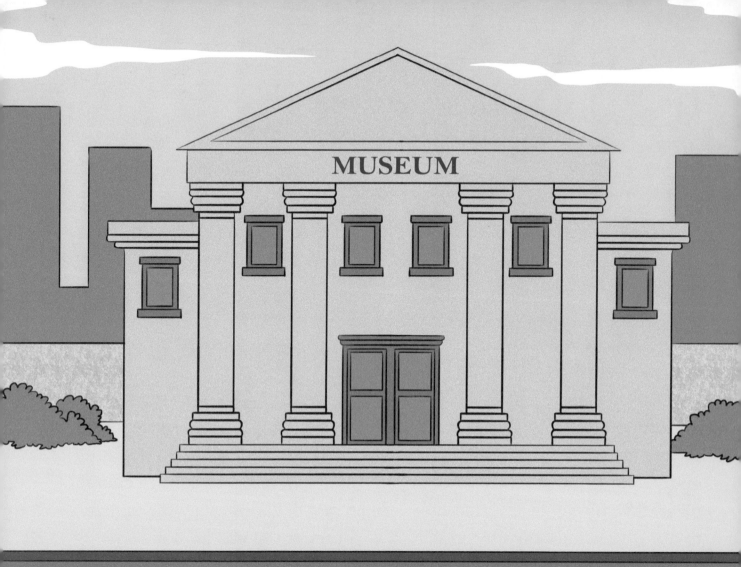

# 6
## chapter

The next day was Thursday. We went to the museum. We noticed that there were lots of police officers and there was Chief too, who was talking to the chief of London's police. Emily and I went to the back exit in case they came out from the back exit.

Emily and I had guns, and Emily had handcuffs too. After one hour people started to come and the crowd stared getting bigger. More and more police officers also were coming because there were so many people. "Hello," someone said really loudly. It was one of the Drake brothers in the museum. And he said again, "I'm Mark. I'm one of the Drake brothers." He got into his car and drove off. The chief said to all police officers, "Get into your cars and follow him." And all the people ran away.

The three other Drake brothers came into the museum dressed like police officers. Emily and I heard glass shatter, so we ran to the front where the diamond was. We saw the Drake brothers. We shouted and asked them to put the diamond on the ground and put their hands in the air.

After an exchange of fire between us and the Drake brothers, Emily was able to handcuff them, and we waited until the other police officers got back. They also caught the fourth Drake brother, Mark, a.k.a. Bob. The other police officers took them to jail.

It was Friday. Emily and I went back to Canada. The next day, I went to work. Suddenly, a loud voice came from the loudspeaker. It was chief. He said, "Emma can you please report to my office." After I heard this, I had mixed emotions, I was feeling happy, nervous and scared at the same time. But I went to the office. "Emma you might be wondering why I called you here today. Well let me tell you since you were able to arrest the drake brothers who we have been trying to arrest for years, I am promoting you to the post of chief," chief said. "Thank you chief but what about you, you are the chief," I asked. "I will be retiring, and I have been looking for some one to take my place and you are the one I want you to take my place," said chief. "Thank you chief I wont let you down," I said.

Later that day, I called Emily and told her the good news. She was so happy for me.

CPSIA information can be obtained
at www.ICGtesting.com
Printed in the USA
BVHW021956150821
614247BV00002B/4